Beautiful Brown Eyes

by

Marianne Richmond

Beautiful Brown Eyes

Marianne Richmond Studios, Inc.
3900 Stinson Boulevard NE
Minneapolis, MN 55421
www.mariannerichmond.com

ISBN 10: 1-934082-59-7
ISBN 13: 978-1-934082-59-1

Illustrations by Marianne Richmond

Book design by Sara Dare Biscan

Printed by Cimarron
Minneapolis, MN, USA
Second Printing, December 2009

Beautiful Brown Eyes

is dedicated to
Big Brown, Little Brown and
Laying Down Brown — MR

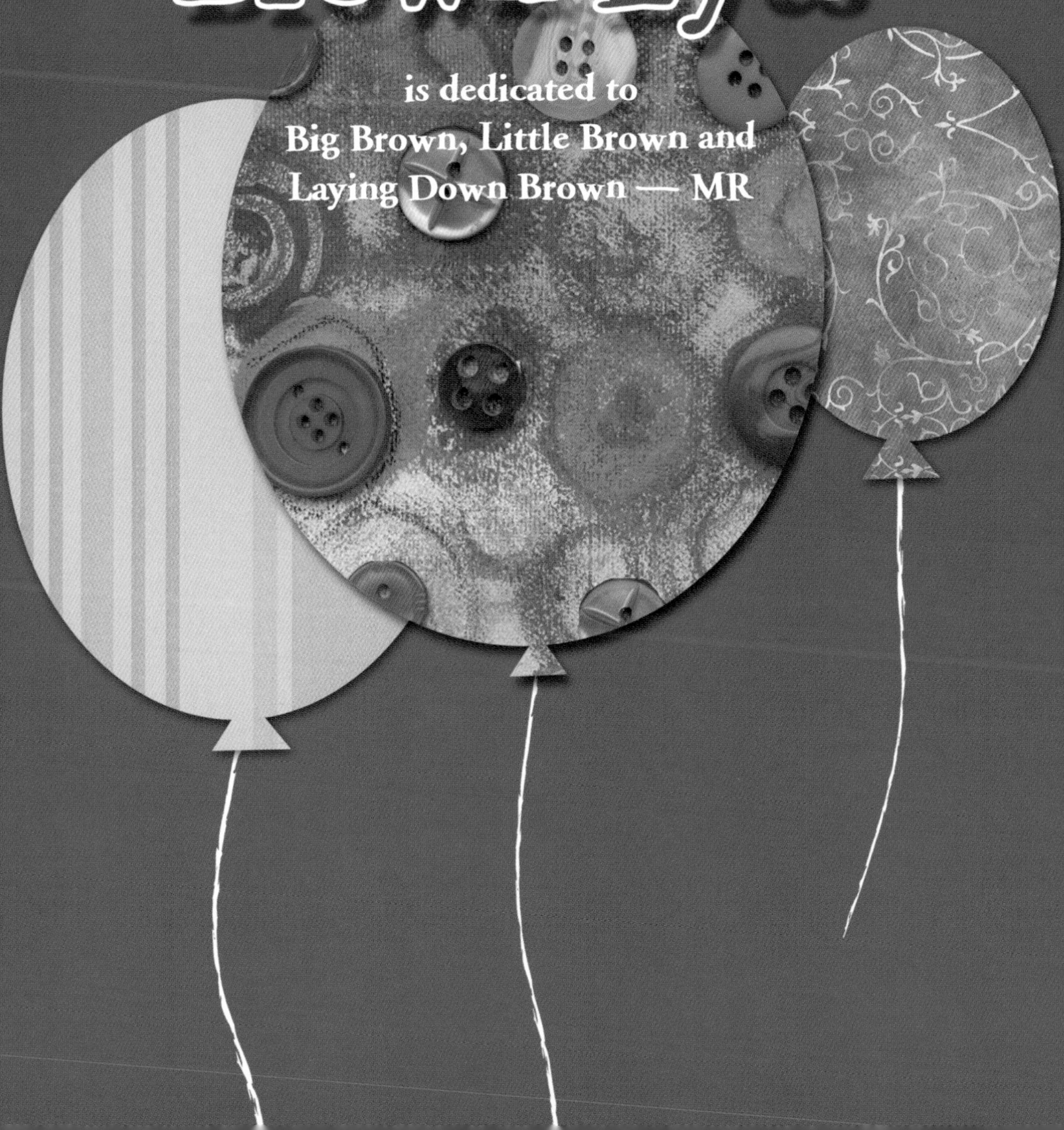

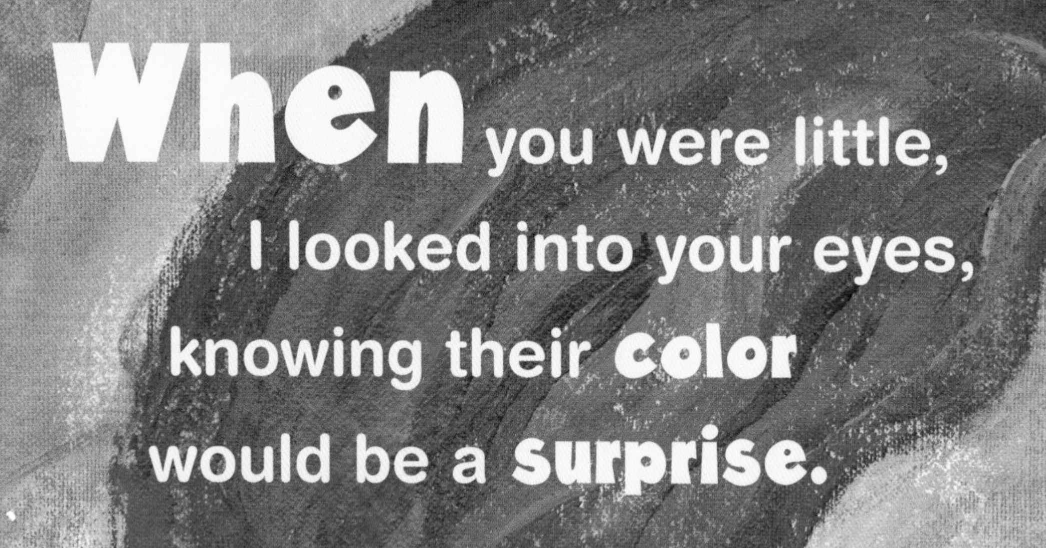

When you were little,
I looked into your eyes,
knowing their **color**
would be a **surprise.**

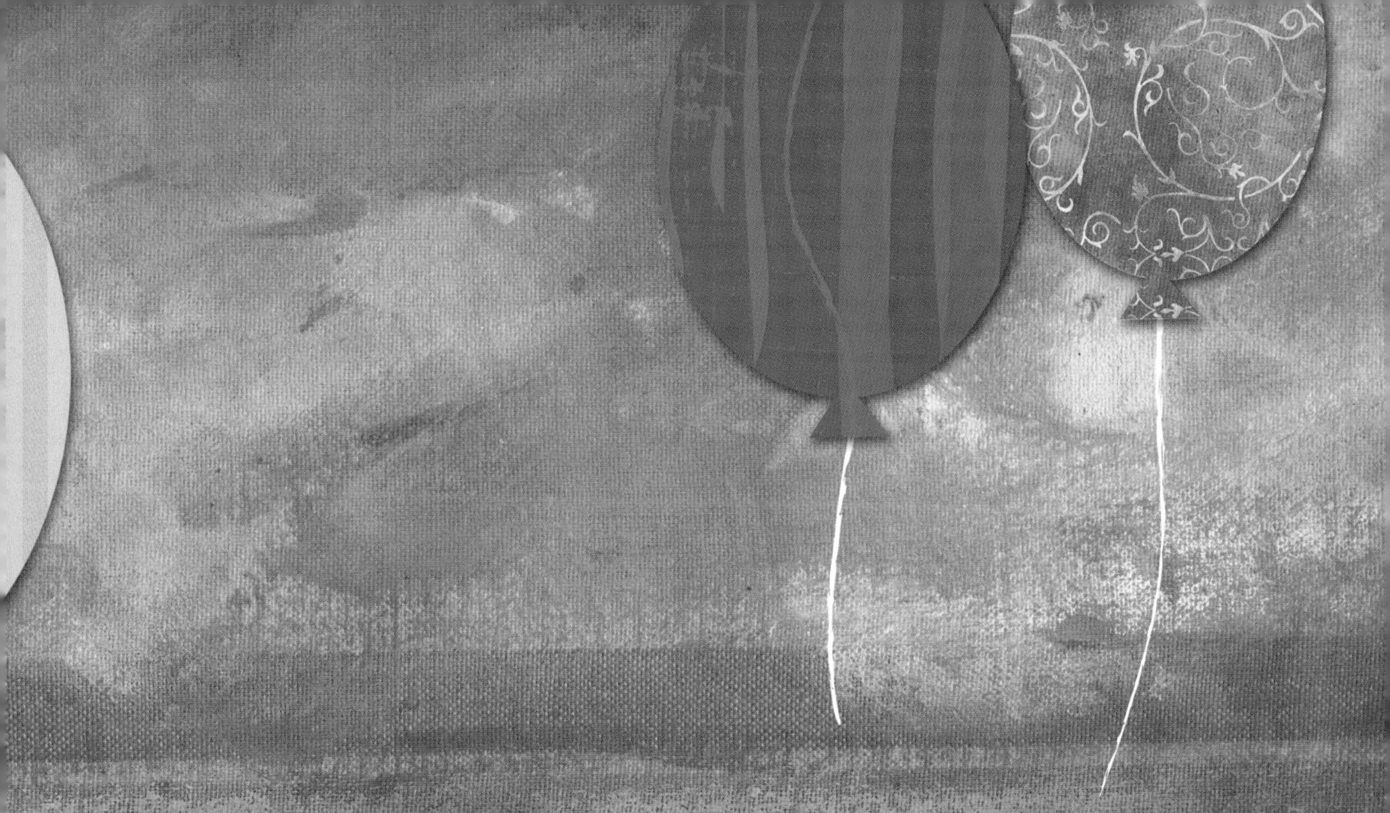

Would they
be **blue** like the sky
or **green** like the earth?
Would they start as one color
and **change** after birth?

I watched and I waited
as your eyes looked 'round,
deciding in time
on their **beautiful brown**.

Brown as **dark chocolate**

or warm **cinnamon toast.**

Brown as the
teddy whom
you love the most.

Lovely, for sure,

those "**browns**" I know,

and, *oh*, what they tell me

about you as you grow.

"Eyes cannot talk!"

you say to me.

"Mouths are for **talking**,

eyes are to **see!"**

Absolutely,

without a doubt.

I see **in**, and you see **out.**

But while I'm looking,

guess what I SEE?

I see your eyes

speaking to me.

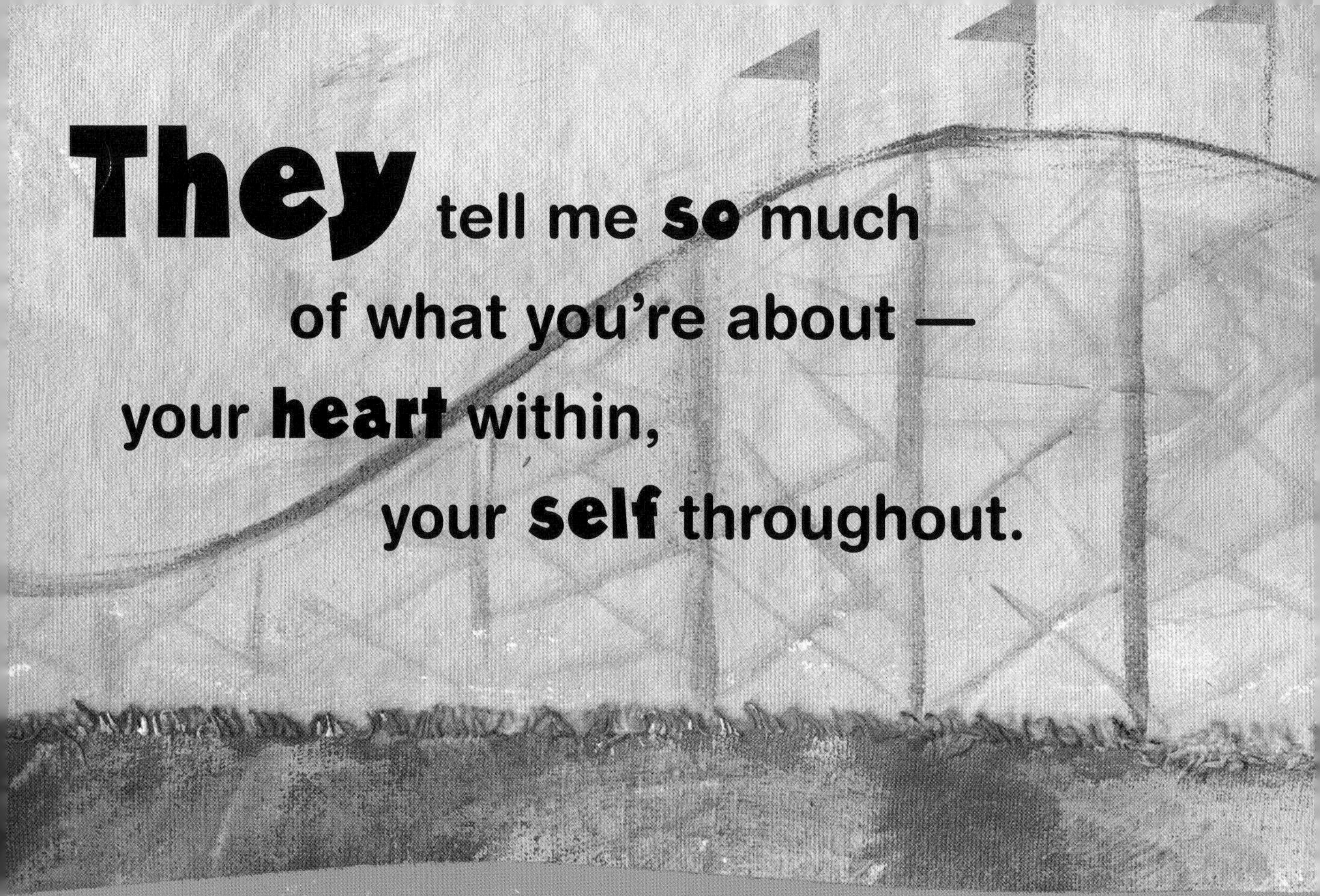

They tell me **so** much
of what you're about —
your **heart** within,
your **self** throughout.

Your **thoughts** and **ways**
and **moods** each one.
Some up, some down,
some "blah," some fun.

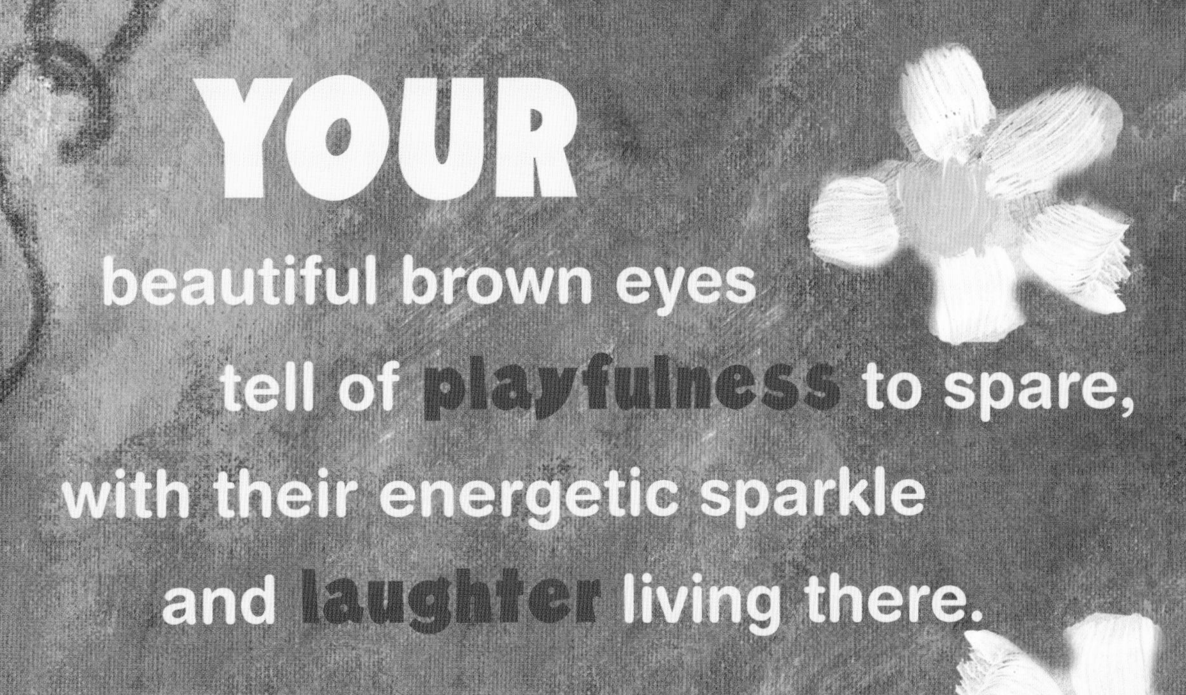

YOUR

beautiful brown eyes
tell of **playfulness** to spare,
with their energetic sparkle
and **laughter** living there.

They show me **creativity**
when you think and play,

growing wide with inspiration
and ideas for your day!

Your

beautiful brown eyes
tell of your **kindness** for sure,
with their gentle **sincerity**
and golden light pure.

"How about when I'm **mad?"** you ask.

"Do my eyes show **crabby***, too?*

Do they tell you when I'm **sorry,**

or when I'm feeling **blue***?"*

Yes, all those and more,

your beautiful **"browns"** say,

telling me in a look

what your voice may never say.

beautiful brown eyes

show your **determination**

to do it, have it, change it,

no matter the situation.

They tell me of your **curiosity**
in questions that you ask.

"Why do grasshoppers hop?"
"Why is nighttime black?"

And when tears spill out,
your "**browns**" tell, too,
of your **empathy** and **sadness**
about some thing or some who.

"My eyes talk **a lot**" you say,
"without me knowing
the happy or sad
they can be showing."

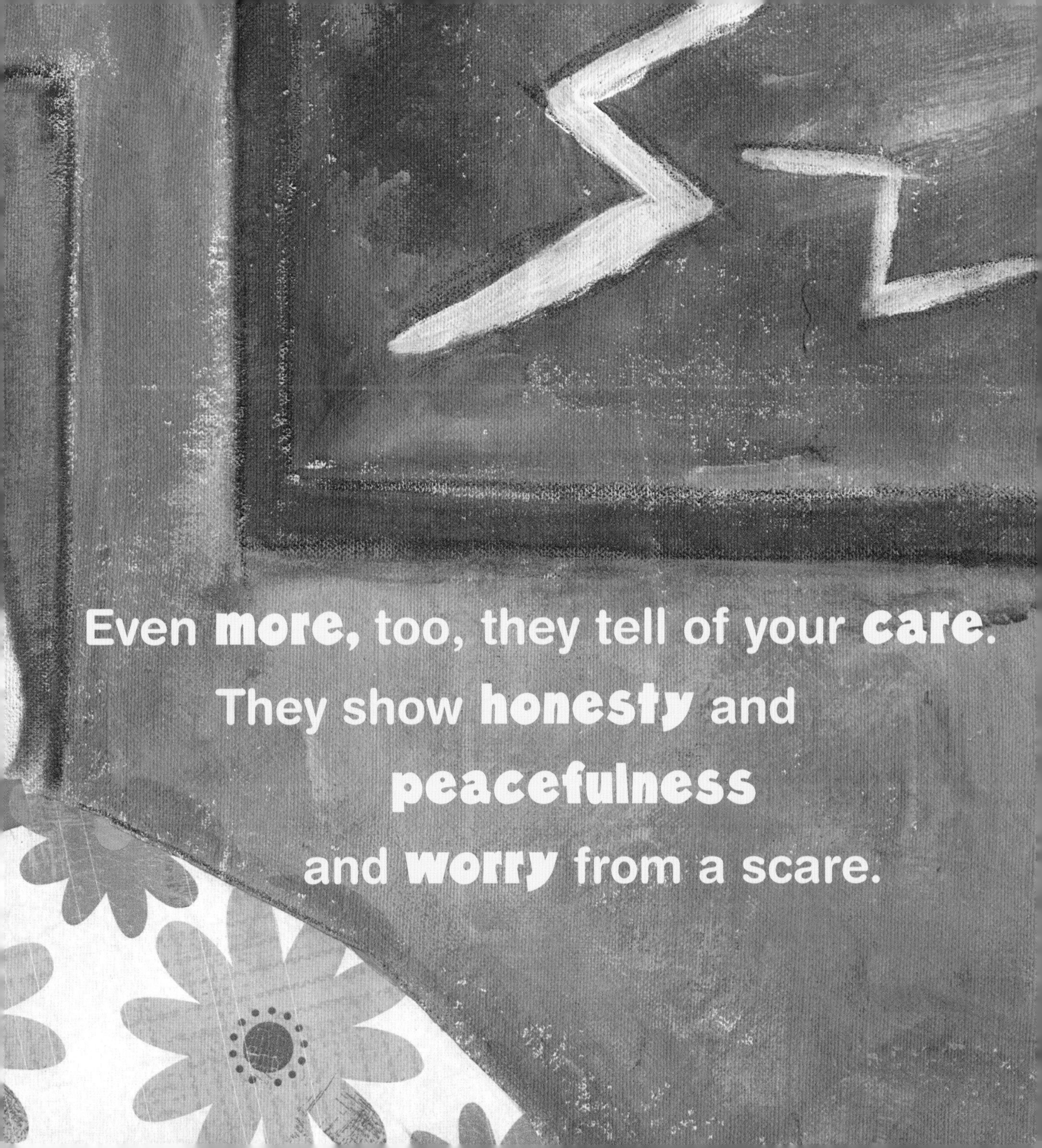

Even **more,** too, they tell of your **care**.
They show **honesty** and
peacefulness
and **worry** from a scare.

Two of my favorite eyes, still,

*(though **you** may not agree)*

tell me of your **sleepiness**

as they blink next to me.

It's then I feel **thankful,**
that I shared another day
with your beautiful brown eyes,
and **all** they do say.